The Monster under the shed

Illustrated by Richard Courtney

Random House 🏠 New York

A Random House PICTUREBACK® Book

Thomas the Tank Engine & Friends A BRITT ALLCROFT COMPANY PRODUCTION Based on The Railway Series by the Rev W Awdry. Copyright © Gullane (Thomas) LLC 2001. All rights reserved under International and Pan-American Copyright Conventions. Published in the United States by Random House, Inc., New York, and simultaneously in Canada by Random House of Canada Limited, Toronto.

www.randomhouse.com/kids   www.thomasthetankengine.com

Library of Congress Cataloging-in-Publication Data
Awdry, W. The monster under the shed / illustrated by Richard Courtney. p. cm. —
(A Random House pictureback book) "Based on the Railway series by the Rev. W. Awdry" — T.p. verso.
Summary: After James tells a scary story, Thomas the tank engine imagines there is a horrible engine-eating monster coming after him.
ISBN 0-375-81371-3 [1. Monsters—Fiction. 2. Railroads—Trains—Fiction. 3. Fear—Fiction. 4. Imagination—Fiction.]
I. Courtney, Richard, 1955– II. Awdry, W. Railway series. III. Random House pictureback. PZ7.M76288 2001 [E]—dc21 00-053331
Printed in the United States of America   First Edition September 2001   10 9

It was a dark, blustery evening at the station. Sir Topham Hatt had closed the railway early on account of the weather. The engines were waiting for the signal to return to their sheds.

"Maybe one of us should tell a story to pass the time," Thomas suggested. The other engines looked pleased with Thomas' idea. "I have the perfect story for tonight," James volunteered with a sly grin.

"A long time ago," James began, "there was a brave blue engine who was always eager to help.

"'Blue engine,' the stationmaster asked one night, 'would you go to the end of the tracks to pick up a coach that was left behind?'

"'Of course,' the brave, eager engine replied. And he set out into the dark, foggy night.

"But by the time the little blue engine reached the end of the tracks, the fog was so thick he could hardly see anything.

"'I'll just have to wait until morning,' said the engine to himself. And he settled into an old shed for the night.

"Late that night, the little blue engine awoke to a noise coming from below the shed.

"*Crreeeak*!

"He opened his eyes and saw long fingers reaching for him through the floorboards. There was a monster under the shed! Terrified, the little blue engine raced out of the shed with the horrible engine-eating monster chasing him through the fog."

"Th-then what happened?" Percy asked timidly.

"That's where the story ends," said James. "No one ever heard from that little blue engine again."

"What about the monster?" Percy whispered.

"Don't be silly, Percy," Gordon said with a chuckle. "It's just a story."

"What if that story is true?" Percy asked Thomas on their way to the sheds. "What if the engine-eating monster is out there somewhere right now?"

"Stop being such a scaredy-cat, Percy," Thomas answered. "There are no such things as monsters."

Later that night, after they had settled in for bed, the engines were startled by a terrible racket coming from Percy's shed.

"Gordon, Thomas, help! There's a monster in my shed!" wailed Percy.

Suddenly, James appeared, roaring with laughter. He had been rattling some scrap metal behind the sheds to frighten Percy.

"I'm a monster! I'm a monster!" James shouted.

Percy was embarrassed for making such a fuss.

"It's okay, Percy," said Henry. "Sometimes good imaginations think bad thoughts."

Later that night, Thomas woke with a fright. He heard a strange noise.
Scratch, scratch.
"Stop it, James!" Thomas yelled.
But James was sound asleep.
Scratch, scratch.
"If it's not James, then maybe I really do have a monster under my shed," thought Thomas. And he stayed awake all night just to be safe.

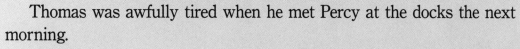

Thomas was awfully tired when he met Percy at the docks the next morning.

"Did you hear any other strange noises in your shed last night?" Thomas asked.

"Not after James' silly prank," Percy replied.

Now Thomas felt silly himself for staying awake all night.

By the middle of the day, Thomas was very sleepy and running far behind schedule. Henry pulled up beside him.

"You look as if you could use some special coal," said Henry.

"Oh, I'm just a little tired," Thomas answered. He didn't want anyone to know that he'd been too frightened to sleep.

Just then, James sped by on the express track.
"What's the matter, Thomas?" he called. "Monsters keeping you up at night?"
And James disappeared down the track, laughing loudly.

By the end of the day, Thomas barely had enough steam to make it back to the yard. The other engines were telling stories again, but Thomas headed straight to bed.

Sometime that night, Thomas woke with a fright.

Scratch, scratch.

The noises were back, and they were definitely coming from under the shed.

"Who's there?" Thomas whispered into the dark.

Crreeeak, crreeeak came the answer.

"Go away, monster. Get out!" Thomas ordered as he closed his eyes tight.

Thump, thump!
Thump, thump!

The noise was getting louder—and *closer*!

"That will surely wake the other engines," Thomas said to himself. "They'll save me from the monster."

But the other engines didn't stir.

Thump, thump.
"It's just outside the door," Thomas yelped. "There's its head!"
"Help, Gordon," Thomas whispered.
But only the monster heard him.
Thump, thump! Thump, thump!

Then the doors of Thomas' shed began to rattle on their hinges.
BANG, BANG, BANG, BANG!
"It's trying to get in!" thought Thomas.
Then, suddenly, the banging stopped.

Thomas was too frightened to move. He peered out into the dark. And
there it was—the horrible engine-eating monster! Thomas could see its
eyes glowing in the night.

Thomas clamped his own eyes shut and screamed.
"Gordon, Henry, Percy, James," he cried. "Save me from THE MONSTER!"

"Thomas," Gordon said, laughing, "open your eyes."

"What are you laughing at, Gordon?" snapped Thomas. "There's a monster right outside my shed!"

"Not anymore," Gordon replied. "Now the monster is *inside* your shed."

Thomas opened one eye very slowly.

"A hedgehog?" Thomas yelled in surprise. "I was afraid of a tiny little hedgehog?"

Now the engines all laughed, and Thomas laughed with them.

"Percy has a good imagination, Thomas, but I think yours is even better," said Gordon with a little chuckle.

"I think you're right," agreed Thomas. "It's the only thing in the world that could turn a tiny hedgehog into a big scary monster."

THE TURTLE SHIP

BY HELENA KU RHEE

ILLUSTRATED BY COLLEEN KONG-SAVAGE

Shen's Books, *an imprint of* Lee & Low Books Inc.
New York

Long ago in Korea, a boy named Sun-sin lived in a small village near the sea. Very few children lived nearby, so sometimes Sun-sin felt lonely.

Sun-sin did have one good friend. This friend was small and green, and his name was Gobugi, which means "turtle."

Sun-sin and Gobugi enjoyed having swim competitions in the ocean. Gobugi usually won.

They also liked to race on the sand. Sun-sin usually won.

On sunny days, Sun-sin and Gobugi relaxed in the garden. Gobugi snacked on lettuce while Sun-sin watched ships sail across the sea. Sun-sin would tell Gobugi how he wished to explore the world and visit different lands.

Sun-sin didn't know how this could ever happen. "I'm just a little boy, and we can't afford to travel," he said to Gobugi.

Gobugi didn't answer, but Sun-sin saw wisdom in the turtle's face and patience in his slow, steady movements. Sun-sin decided to be wise and patient too.

One day, an important announcement arrived from the royal palace. In a month, the king would hold a contest to find the best design for a new battleship to defend the land. Anyone could enter the contest. The winner would earn ten bags of copper coins and sail the ocean with the royal navy.

Sun-sin wanted to travel. He wanted to explore the world. He knew he had to try to design the greatest battleship!

Sun-sin found tree branches and tied them with twine to make a raft. Then he took it to the water and placed Gobugi on top. The raft floated until a huge wave crashed down and broke it into splinters.

Gobugi bobbed on the surface of the water and made it safely to shore.

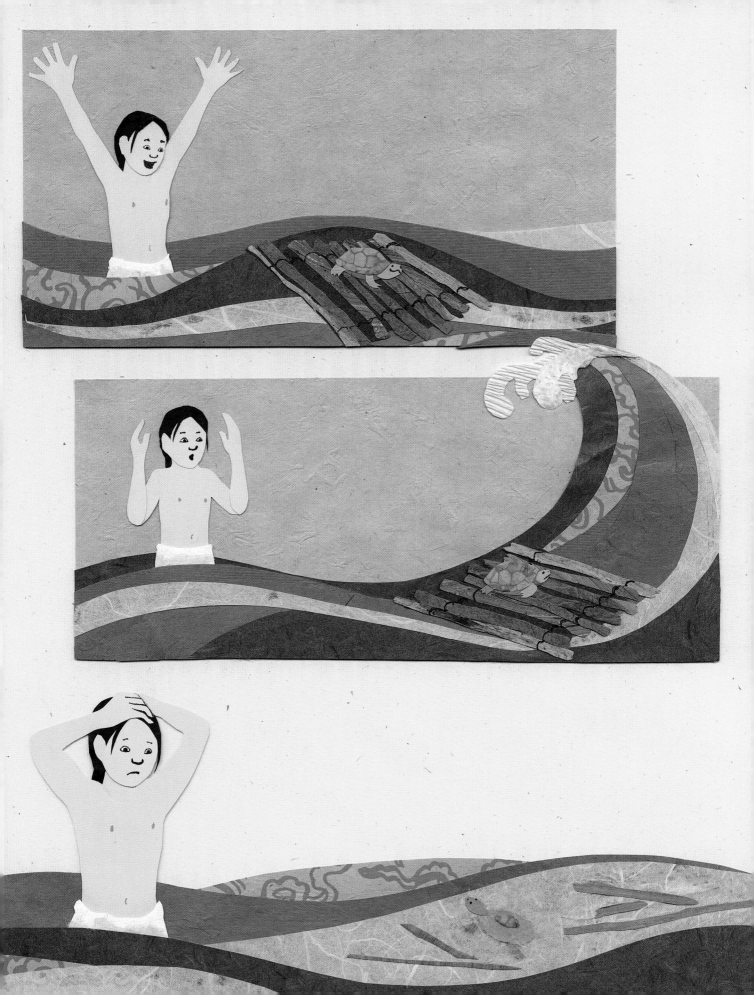

The next day, Sun-sin made a stronger ship. He found logs, laid them side by side, and tied them together with rope. He used mud to stick tiles along the edges to make a barrier against the waves. When the mud dried, he placed Gobugi on the ship. Using all his strength, Sun-sin pulled it to the water. The boat looked sturdy as it glided away. Sun-sin was sure no waves would break through this time.

It wasn't long before water filled the boat and it started to sink. The ship was too heavy!

Gobugi floated on the waves and made it safely to shore.

That's when Sun-sin noticed that his turtle was small but mighty, slow but steady. Gobugi was an excellent swimmer and impossible to sink. Suddenly, Sun-sin had an idea for a battleship.

Sun-sin begged his parents to let him enter the contest.

"*No!*" said his father. "The king will never listen to a little boy with a pet turtle."

But Sun-sin reminded his parents that anyone could enter the contest. "And if I win," he said, "we'll have enough money to buy food for an entire year and cotton to make new clothes. We could even buy shrimp for Gobugi!"

His parents finally agreed. They traveled on foot for days through valleys and forests. They passed rivers, lakes, and streams.

At last, they arrived at the royal palace. It was the most majestic building Sun-sin had ever seen.

Sun-sin and his family stood among hundreds of people who had drawings and models of battleships. Each ship was bigger and better than the next.

Some people stared at Sun-sin and whispered, "Why is that child here with a turtle? He should go home and play with his friends!"

When it was finally his turn to present to the king, Sun-sin and his parents got on their knees and bowed deeply. Sun-sin was terribly nervous. He didn't know what to say.

One of the king's counselors yelled, "Hurry up, boy! You're wasting our time."

Sun-sin gathered all his courage, and with his head still bowed, he held Gobugi up to the king. In a loud voice he said, "Your Highness, my turtle is strong and steady and never sinks. A battleship designed like this turtle will protect our land from invaders."

The king's counselors laughed and laughed.

One counselor said, "That's the puniest turtle I've ever seen! Let's throw it in the soup for dinner!"

Another said, "A turtle is the slowest creature in the sea. A shark would eat it in two seconds!"

Embarrassed, Sun-sin's parents led him away. Gobugi trailed after them.

Suddenly a cat leaped through the air! It pounced onto Gobugi's
back, but the turtle's slippery shell made the cat tumble to the floor.
Then it bit at Gobugi, but the turtle's armor was too tough to crack.
The cat swiped Gobugi with its sharp claws, but the turtle hid deep
within his shell, tucking his limbs safely inside.

Defeated, the cat ran away.

Sun-sin checked on his friend. Slowly, the turtle moved
his arms and legs. He poked out his head and wiggled his tail.
Gobugi was perfectly fine.

The people applauded. "Hooray! What a mighty little turtle!
Hooray!"

The king approached Sun-sin. "Your turtle is indeed strong
and steady. A ship designed like this turtle will surely protect our
kingdom from invaders."

The king awarded Sun-sin ten bags of copper coins, and the next day, he ordered the royal navy to start building the battleship. The king named the vessel *Gobukson*, which means "Turtle Ship."

Just like Gobugi, the Turtle Ship was small but strong. The ship was made of wood and covered in iron plating and sheets of spiked metal. The deck's covering was curved like a turtle's shell. Rows of long, sturdy oars stuck out of the lower deck and could be pulled into the ship's body. At the back, the stern was in the shape of a tail. Instead of a turtle's head, the navy added a dragon's head to scare its enemies.

The king loved the design of the Turtle Ship and ordered the navy to build more.

After the first Turtle Ship was built, the king remembered his promise. Sun-sin and his family were invited to travel with the royal navy to different lands.

Many years later, Sun-sin became a navy admiral. During one famous battle, Sun-sin led thirteen Turtle Ships against one hundred thirty invader ships. The Turtle Ships defeated all of them!

The Turtle Ships went on to defend the kingdom for many years. The people enjoyed great peace and prosperity during this time. Sun-sin and the Turtle Ships were celebrated across the land and beyond.

And yet, no matter how many people he met, no matter how many places he visited, Sun-sin discovered he was happiest to be in the garden with his old friend Gobugi, watching ships sail across the sea.

AFTERWORD

This story is loosely based on Korean history. During the 1500s, Admiral Yi Sun-sin (pronounced "ee soon-shin") improved an existing battleship design to create Korea's famed Turtle Ship, known as *Gobukson* (pronounced "guh-book-son"). Korea's royal navy used the warship during the Joseon dynasty, which lasted from the early fifteenth century until the nineteenth century. The ship's name derives from its protective ironclad covering, reminiscent of a turtle's shell. At one time, scholars believed the first ironclad ships were European or American (such as the USS *Monitor* and CSS *Virginia*, used during the Civil War), but the Turtle Ship is dated hundreds of years earlier.

Fully covered with metal sheets, the Turtle Ship's deck deflected fire arrows and musket shots. Straw thatching camouflaged iron spikes that poked out of the deck, so adversaries who jumped on board landed in a deadly trap. The prow of the battleship resembled the head of a dragon, perhaps the most feared creature in Asia at that time. This allowed the royal navy to wage psychological warfare on its enemies. The dragon's head was large enough to house a cannon, and sailors shot sulfurous smoke through the dragon's mouth to repel adversaries while also concealing the ship's movements during close combat. Below the dragon's head, each Turtle Ship had a large wooden gargoyle, allowing the ship to ram into enemy vessels without critical damage to its body.

Photo courtesy of the War Memorial of Korea

The Turtle Ship's relatively small size—it was approximately 100 to 120 feet long—allowed it to hide among tall waves. Each ship had two masts, two sails, and ten or more long oars, which enabled deft maneuvering in the water. It could easily change directions, and could stop, pivot and move backward, like a turtle in the sea. The ship could even rotate on its radius, much like a helicopter does today. And though the ship was not the fastest vessel on the sea, it was capable of sudden bursts of speed.

AUTHOR'S NOTE

Both the illustrator and I conducted extensive research for this book, but ultimately, this is a work of fiction. Therefore, some creative liberties were taken in the depiction of Admiral Yi Sun-sin's life and the time period in both the text and illustrations to dramatize the story for young readers. For instance, historians debate whether the Turtle Ship sailed in every big battle, and if there were thirteen Turtle Ships against more than one hundred enemy ships during the Battle of Myeongnyang, as described in the story. However, stories told by my parents and family featured the Turtle Ship as an ever-present symbol of strength and resilience, and this book was inspired by their magnificent tales. For resources that present a more historically accurate account, please refer to the materials noted in the bibliography.

ILLUSTRATOR'S NOTE

My studio gets hit by a paper blizzard when I illustrate in collage. Snips of colors and patterns blanket the table and floor. Each picture is a carefully balanced palette of colors, textures, and decorative designs. The way I juxtapose these elements affects how the viewer reads the composition: contrasting hues make shapes pop off the page, patterns make interesting accents, textured papers suggest an object's rough surface. I use a magnifying lamp to draw or cut the smallest parts, then tweezers to handle those pieces because human fingers are too big and clumsy.

The papers used for the illustrations in this book are from around the world. I used Korean hanji in the landscape, Egyptian papyrus for the Turtle Ships, Mexican Amate as the court floors, and Italian crepe for the pine needles. I smile to think that at the beginning of the story Sun-sin itches to explore distant lands, never knowing that in this book he is already surrounded by bits of Thailand, Nepal, India, France, Japan, and more.

For my wonderful family of storytellers—H.K.R.

For Noah, who inspires me—C.K-S.

Bibliography

Cumings, Bruce. *Korea's Place in the Sun: A Modern History.* New York: W. W. Norton, 1997.

Diamond Sutra Recitation Group. *Admiral Yi Sun-sin: A Brief Overview of His Life and Achievements.* Seoul, South Korea: Korean Spirit & Culture Promotion Project, 2008.

Jo, Seong-do. *Admiral Yi Sun-Sin: A National Hero of Korea.* Revised and enlarged by Korean Naval Academy Museum. Seoul, South Korea: Sinseowon, 2005.

Text copyright © 2018 by Helena Ku Rhee
Illustrations copyright © 2018 by Colleen Kong-Savage
All rights reserved. No part of this book may be reproduced, transmitted, or stored in
an information retrieval system in any form or by any means, electronic, mechanical, photocopying,
recording, or otherwise, without written permission from the publisher.
Shen's Books, an imprint of LEE & LOW BOOKS Inc., 95 Madison Avenue, New York, NY 10016
leeandlow.com
Edited by Jessica V. Echeverria
Designed by Christy Hale
Production by The Kids at Our House
The text is set in Goudy Old Style
The illustrations are rendered in collage

Manufactured in Malaysia by Tien Wah Press
10 9 8 7 6 5 4 3 2 1
First Edition

Library of Congress Cataloging-in-Publication Data
Names: Rhee, Helena Ku, author. | Kong-Savage, Colleen, illustrator.
Title: The Turtle Ship / by Helena Ku Rhee; illustrated by Colleen Kong-Savage.
Description: First edition. | New York: Shen's Books, an imprint of Lee & Low Books Inc., [2018]
Summary: An adaptation of the legend of Sun-sin Yi, a young boy in sixteenth-century Korea,
who, inspired by his pet turtle, designs one of the greatest battleships in history
and fulfills his dream of sailing the world.
Identifiers: LCCN 2017053263 | ISBN 9781885008909 (hardback)
Subjects: LCSH: Yi, Sun-sin, 1545-1598—Legends. | CYAC: Yi, Sun-sin,
1545-1598—Legends. | Folklore—Korea. | Battleships—Folklore. |Ships—Folklore.
Classification: LCC PZ8.1.R373 Tu 2018 | DDC 398.2 [E]—dc23
LC record available at https://lccn.loc.gov/2017053263